the IRISH CINDERLAD

By Shirley Climo
Illustrated by Loretta Krupinski

HarperCollins*Publishers*

Library of Congress Cataloging-in-Publication Data
Climo, Shirley.
  The Irish Cinderlad / by Shirley Climo; illustrated by Loretta Krupinski.
     p.   cm.
  Summary: Becan, a poor boy belittled by his stepmother and stepsisters, rescues a
princess in distress after meeting a magical bull.
     ISBN 0-06-024396-1. — ISBN 0-06-024397-X (lib. bdg.)
     [1. Fairy tales   2. Folklore—Ireland.]   I. Krupinski, Loretta, ill.
II. Title.
PZ8.C56Ir   1996   94-37545
[398.2'0941502]—dc20   CIP
                                                                        AC

1 2 3 4 5 6 7 8 9 10

First Edition

For George who took me to Ireland
and then took me back again
—S.C.

In Ireland, in the old times, there lived a lad named Becan. His mother gave him this name the day he was born, for Becan is Irish for "Little One."

"It's fitting," said she, "for such a wee thing."

His mother loved him all the same and carried Becan about in her egg basket for safekeeping. Whenever he opened his mouth, she spooned milk porridge into it, and Becan began to grow. Red hair flamed on his head. His skinny legs got rounder, and his tiny feet got longer until his toes poked out of the basket.

Although the rest of him stayed small, his feet kept on growing. By the time Becan was thirteen years old, they were so large he'd splash a puddle dry just by stepping in it. Still, Becan's worries were few enough until his mother died.

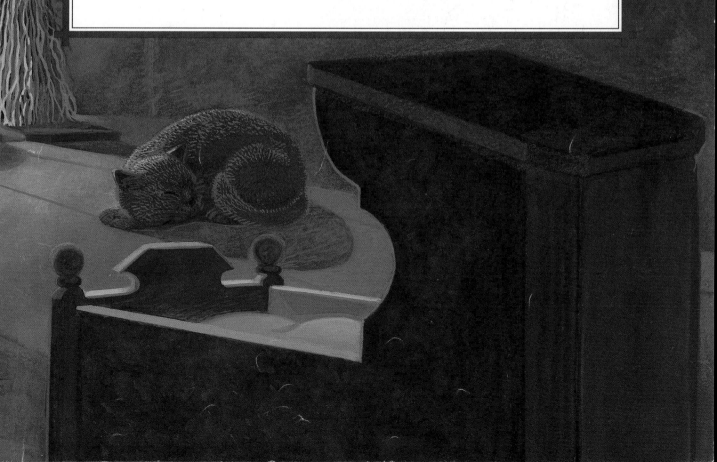

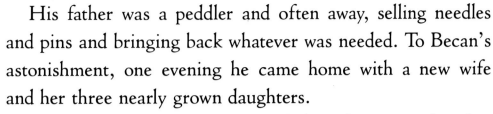

His father was a peddler and often away, selling needles and pins and bringing back whatever was needed. To Becan's astonishment, one evening he came home with a new wife and her three nearly grown daughters.

"Now you've a mam again, and three big sisters besides, to watch out for you," his father explained.

Watch they did. All three sisters spied on him, and if anything went amiss, they shrieked, "Blame Little Bigfoot!" for that is what they called him.

"We'd be better off without that good-for-nothing boy," said their mother.

At last, she told Becan, "Your big feet are always in the way! It's time you went off to tend to the cows."

"Cows are fine company," Becan replied, "but I've heard talk of a mean speckled bull. A kick from him can send a man sailing over the rainbow."

"Stop fretting," snapped his stepmother. "Not even a cow could mistake *you* for a man."

So Becan became a herdboy. Each day at sunup, he led his father's three cows up the hill to graze on purple clover. At sundown, he brought them home again. In between, he sat under an oak tree and kept a sharp eye out for the speckled bull.

One misty morning, Becan heard a bellow louder than a thunderclap. Rocks rattled down the hill, cows galloped about in circles, and Becan scampered up the oak tree. When he dared to look, it was right into the angry eyes of an enormous bull.

The creature's face was white, but splashed with rusty red like the freckles on Becan's nose. The hoofs were big and broad like Becan's feet. He twitched his long tail and pawed the ground, ready to knock down the tree and the boy with it. Quickly, Becan stretched out his hand and scratched him behind the ear, in the place that cows like best.

"We could be cousins, you and I," said Becan, jumping down, "for we look to be patched together from the same odds and ends."

The bull lowered his head with the wicked curved horns. But instead of tossing Becan, he nuzzled his cheek. From that moment, the bull and the boy were fast friends. Becan told of his troubles, while the speckled bull listened, chewing thoughtfully.

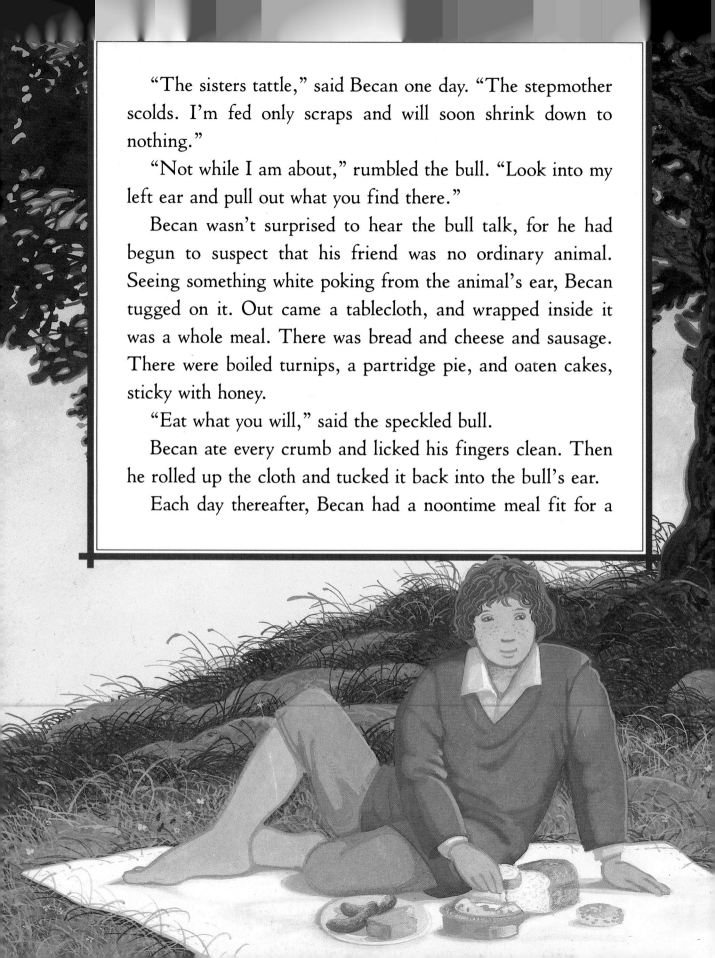

"The sisters tattle," said Becan one day. "The stepmother scolds. I'm fed only scraps and will soon shrink down to nothing."

"Not while I am about," rumbled the bull. "Look into my left ear and pull out what you find there."

Becan wasn't surprised to hear the bull talk, for he had begun to suspect that his friend was no ordinary animal. Seeing something white poking from the animal's ear, Becan tugged on it. Out came a tablecloth, and wrapped inside it was a whole meal. There was bread and cheese and sausage. There were boiled turnips, a partridge pie, and oaten cakes, sticky with honey.

"Eat what you will," said the speckled bull.

Becan ate every crumb and licked his fingers clean. Then he rolled up the cloth and tucked it back into the bull's ear.

Each day thereafter, Becan had a noontime meal fit for a

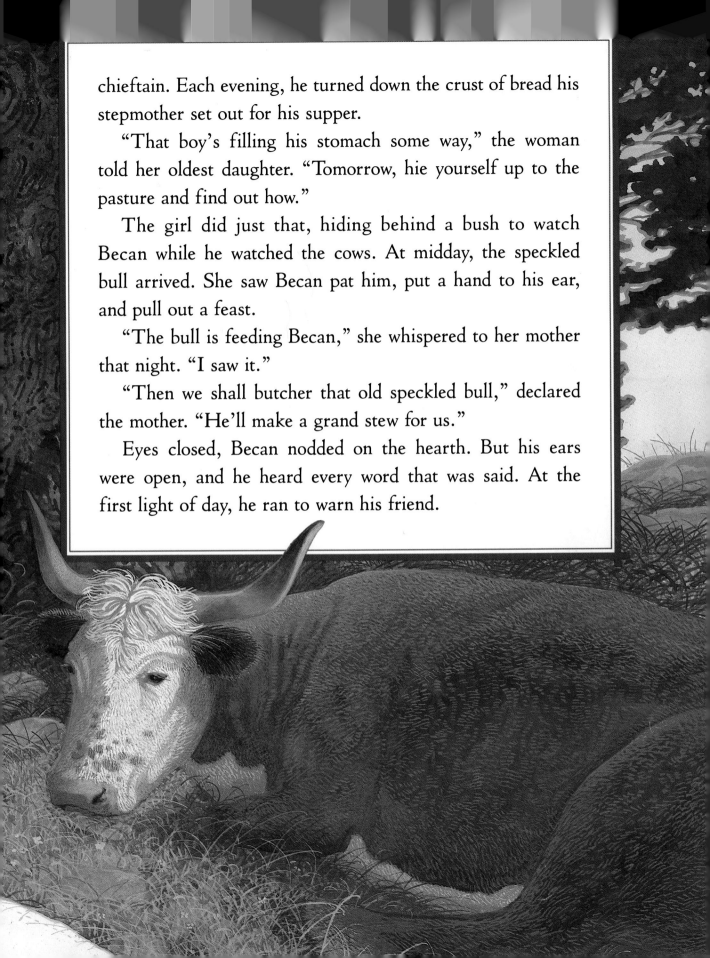

chieftain. Each evening, he turned down the crust of bread his stepmother set out for his supper.

"That boy's filling his stomach some way," the woman told her oldest daughter. "Tomorrow, hie yourself up to the pasture and find out how."

The girl did just that, hiding behind a bush to watch Becan while he watched the cows. At midday, the speckled bull arrived. She saw Becan pat him, put a hand to his ear, and pull out a feast.

"The bull is feeding Becan," she whispered to her mother that night. "I saw it."

"Then we shall butcher that old speckled bull," declared the mother. "He'll make a grand stew for us."

Eyes closed, Becan nodded on the hearth. But his ears were open, and he heard every word that was said. At the first light of day, he ran to warn his friend.

The bull snorted. "I'll not end in a soup pot! Get on my back, lad, and we'll soon be gone from here."

With Becan holding tight to his horns, the bull trotted up the hill, over a steep mountain, and through a wood of beech trees. In a meadow, many days from home, the bull stopped.

"Here we bid good-bye," he said. "For it is here that the gray bull and I must fight."

"No!" Becan threw his arms around the bull's neck.

"The gray bull shall kill me, for my fate has been foretold. When I am dead, you are to twist off my tail."

Becan stared at him in horror. "Never!"

"Wear my tail as a belt. Use it when you need my help the most." The bull nudged Becan gently. "Do as I say."

Early the next morning, a bull, gray as the sky overhead, came charging through the trees. The two bulls locked horns and fought throughout the rainy day. When evening came, the gray bull had disappeared and the speckled bull lay dead.

Becan sat beside his friend all night. At dawn, remembering the bull's words, he cautiously twisted his tail. It spun around in a full circle and came off at once.

Becan wrapped the tail twice about his waist and then, for the last time, reached into the animal's ear. He pulled out the tablecloth, now bare of food and fresh as new, and carefully covered the bull.

"Slán," he whispered, which is the Irish word for good-bye.

Alone, Becan continued his journey, walking down a rocky ridge and into a valley. The stones cut his bare feet, and he was grateful when a gentleman on horseback offered him a ride.

"Where are you bound, lad?" the man asked.

Becan shrugged. "I'm going anywhere at all."

"You could come along with me," the gentleman suggested. "I am in want of a cowherd."

"Herding is what I do best," answered Becan.

"I've this horse, four cows, three sheep, and a donkey, and all of them good-natured. What's bad-tempered is on the other side of my wall . . . an *arhach*."

"A giant!" Becan exclaimed. "I'd like to see one."

"Take warning." The gentleman waggled his finger. "My last herdboy, a lad far bigger and stronger than you . . . "

Although he knew quite well what was meant, Becan said at once, "I'll have the job anyway, if it please you."

Becan became a herder again, sleeping in a cowshed by night and taking the horse, the cows, the sheep, and the donkey out to graze by day. When they had chomped and chewed up everything in the gentleman's field, Becan climbed the stone wall to see what grew on the other side. Before him spread acres of grassy meadows and orchards of apple trees bowed with fruit.

Becan knocked stones from the wall until it was low enough for the animals to step over. "Help yourselves," he told them. "That arhach has so much, he won't mind sharing." Then Becan climbed a tree to pick an apple for himself.

"Got you!" a voice bellowed.

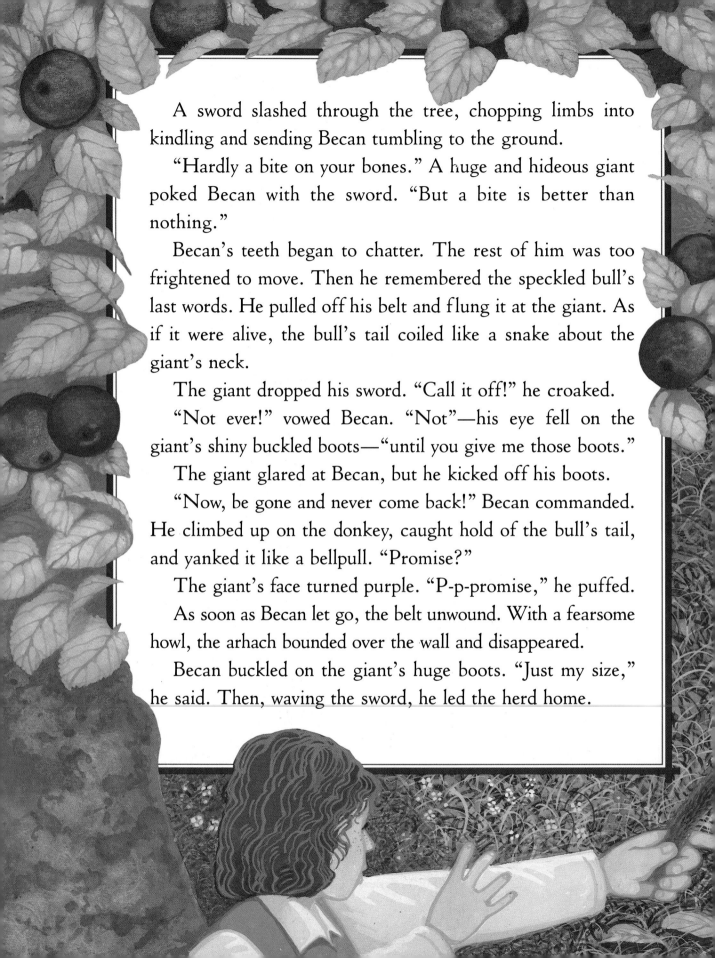

A sword slashed through the tree, chopping limbs into kindling and sending Becan tumbling to the ground.

"Hardly a bite on your bones." A huge and hideous giant poked Becan with the sword. "But a bite is better than nothing."

Becan's teeth began to chatter. The rest of him was too frightened to move. Then he remembered the speckled bull's last words. He pulled off his belt and flung it at the giant. As if it were alive, the bull's tail coiled like a snake about the giant's neck.

The giant dropped his sword. "Call it off!" he croaked.

"Not ever!" vowed Becan. "Not"—his eye fell on the giant's shiny buckled boots—"until you give me those boots."

The giant glared at Becan, but he kicked off his boots.

"Now, be gone and never come back!" Becan commanded. He climbed up on the donkey, caught hold of the bull's tail, and yanked it like a bellpull. "Promise?"

The giant's face turned purple. "P-p-promise," he puffed.

As soon as Becan let go, the belt unwound. With a fearsome howl, the arhach bounded over the wall and disappeared.

Becan buckled on the giant's huge boots. "Just my size," he said. Then, waving the sword, he led the herd home.

Some time later, the gentleman told Becan, "Stay home with the cows today. There's trouble coming to the town of Kinsale."

"Trouble?" asked Becan.

"'Tis the Day of the Dragon." His master shuddered. "Every seven years, that wicked lizard rises from the ocean and swallows the fairest maiden in the land."

"And what if she does not care for that?" Becan asked.

"Oh, she has no choice, for she'll be bound to a post. If she's not there, the dragon will blow the sea onto the land, wash away the village, and drown all the people."

"That *is* trouble indeed!" cried Becan.

"This year the lass is Princess Finola, the king's own daughter." He squinted at Becan. "Don't you be thinking of going. The crowd might crush one as small as you."

Going was just what Becan had in mind. While his master slept, Becan put on the giant's boots and thrust the sword into his bull-tail belt. Then he scrambled up on the donkey and rode off to Kinsale.

Becan spied the king's castle first, for it was perched high on a headland above the blue-green sea. As he trotted down the hillside into town, Becan saw carts crowding the shore and a girl tied to a post at the water's edge. A band of gold circled her shiny black hair, and Becan knew she was Princess Finola.

The scene was strangely silent. Only the voice of the princess was heard over the splash of the waves.

"Will no one help me?" she pleaded.

People looked away from her. Some hung their heads, but none moved.

"I shall!" cried Becan, sliding from the donkey. "Let me sharpen my sword on that dragon. I'll . . . "

"Look behind you!" the princess screamed.

Becan wheeled about. The sea was bubbling, as if coming to a boil, and suddenly a monstrous dragon burst from the water. Flames flashed from its mouth, and its barbed tail churned the waves to a froth. Scales plated its body like armor, and the nails on its toes were sharper than daggers.

Becan raised the giant's sword with trembling hands. "Beware, Serpent!" he shouted, and the battle began.

"Ooooh!" moaned the crowd, as the dragon almost caught Becan in its claws.

"Bravo!" cried the princess, as Becan's sword drew blood.

But the creature acted as if the strikes from the sword were pinpricks. By afternoon, Becan was so tired, he could hardly lift the blade. Grasping his belt instead, he hurled it at the dragon. The bull's tail wrapped itself around the fiery jaws, tying them shut. The dragon snorted and heaved, but each move tightened the belt. Soon only two thin streams of smoke curled from its nostrils. With a sizzle, the monster sank beneath the waves, taking the tail of the speckled bull down with it.

People cheered and rushed to Becan, almost crushing him, just as his master had warned. Then he heard "Little Bigfoot!" and saw his three stepsisters ready to pounce on him like three cats on a mouse. Becan jumped on his donkey.

"Wait!" cried Princess Finola. She reached for Becan and caught him by the boot. "I want to thank you!"

"You're welcome, to be sure." Kicking the donkey, Becan took off down the road as if the dragon still chased him.

And the princess was left holding his boot.

The next day, Becan took his herd to pasture, just as always. But now he had only one boot, his bull-tail belt was gone forever, and the tip of the giant's sword was bent like a fishhook. Becan dug a hole and buried the sword under an apple tree.

"That's the end of it all," he said.

But it wasn't. Princess Finola still had the other boot, and she was determined to find its owner. "I'll marry the one whose foot fits this boot, and none other," she insisted. "It was he and he alone who saved me from the dragon."

The king sent a royal messenger to crisscross the country from sea to mountains with orders to find the owner of the boot. Many wished to wed the pretty dark-haired princess. Soldiers and sailors, fishermen and farmers, all tried on the shoe. Some stuffed the toe with sawdust, others used sheep's wool, and more than a few wore layer upon layer of thick knitted stockings. Still, the boot was too big for any of them.

"'Tis giant-sized," they grumbled.

A year passed before the messenger arrived at the gentleman's house. When Becan's master slipped on the boot, it slipped right off again.

"Let the lad have a go at it," he said.

"A cowherd?" The messenger winked at the gentleman, but he handed the boot to Becan. "Why not?"

Of course, the boot fit Becan as snug as his own skin. He kicked up his heel, grinned at his master, and said to the astonished messenger, "I've the mate to it in the cowshed."

Soon enough, Becan was on his way to Kinsale again, wearing both boots and astride the gentleman's fine horse.

"How grand!" cried the princess when he arrived at the castle. "We're just the same height, sir, so I know we'll see eye to eye on everything."

He grinned at her. "You can call me Becan," he said, "for that's what my mother named me."

"You shall be *Prince* Becan," said Princess Finola. She hugged him, and the lad blushed as red as the hair on his head.

Author's Note

In Ireland, for a thousand years, a seanachaoi, or storyteller, was second only to a king, and Irish harpers sang their ballads in every court. Then, in 1366, an English law, the Statute of Kilkenny, banned bards and poets from using their native tongue. Forbidden or forgotten, few Irish legends or folktales found their way into print until the 1800's. The Irish Cinderlad is an adaptation of one of these old stories revived in the nineteenth century.

A Cinderlad tale isn't unique to Ireland. Around the world, there are many variations of the story. Most familiar is the Scandinavian Askelad, but other European Cinderlads are found in England, Hungary, and the Balkans. India and Japan have similar tales, and the Hausa people of Africa have a hero who is identified by a shoe test.

Like his female counterpart, a male Cinderella is aided by some magical being. Although a bull seems a strange fairy godmother, in long-ago Ireland, cattle were thought to have come from the sea and to have unusual powers. In particular, a cow with a white face and red ears was considered an enchanted creature.

This condensed retelling is based primarily on Douglas Hyde's "The Bracket Bull" (Four Irish Stories, Dublin, 1898) and on Sara Cone Bryant's "Billy Beg and His Bull" (Best Stories to Tell to Children, Houghton Mifflin Co., Cambridge, MA, 1905).